BOBBY'S WORLD™
Sleepover Scare

Based on characters created by Howie Mandel
Adapted by Ronald Kidd
Illustrations by Tom Brenner and Kelley Jarvis

Bedrock Press

Did I ever tell you about the time I won the Indy 500 car race?

It was near the end of the race, and there were two cars ahead of me.

I passed one of them on the turn, and the crowd went wild.

"Who is this kid?" they kept asking. "How can he possibly be so great?"

There was just one car left ahead of me. I shot past it and zoomed across the finish line! "Bobby! Bobby! Bobby!" the crowd chanted.

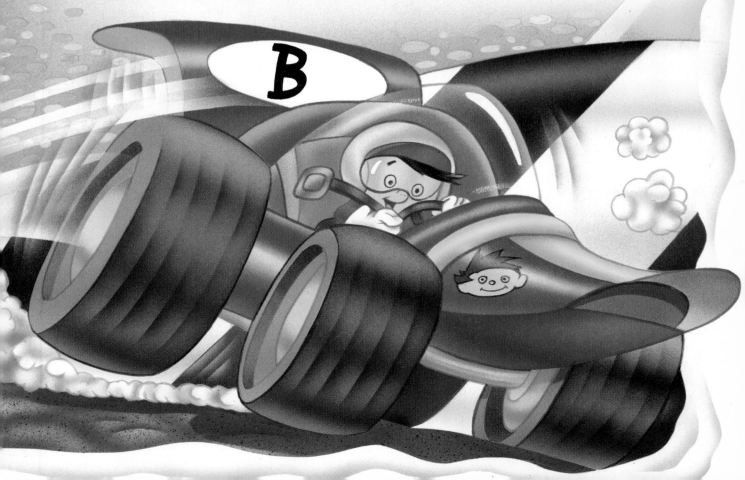

"It's nothing," I said. "It's nothing," I repeated to my new friend, Gordon. We weren't really at the Indy 500. We were playing in my room one Saturday afternoon.

"Nothing?" said Gordon. "This picture of a race car is great! Bobby, you're the best drawer I know. I'm your number one fan."

"You are?"

"Sure!" he said. "Hey, you want to sleep over at my house tonight?"

It sounded like fun to me. But if I slept at his house, where was he going to sleep?

We asked my mom, and she told me it was called a sleepover. I would sleep at Gordon's house, and so would he!

I hurried upstairs to pack, and my mom came up a few minutes later to see how I was doing. "For corn sakes," she said, checking my bag, "where are your PJs and your toothbrush?"

How was I supposed to pack PJs and a toothbrush when there wasn't even room for all my toys?

We finally got my bag packed, and Uncle Ted drove me to Gordon's house. On the way over, he grinned and said the same thing he always says.

"Hey, Bobbo, you know what time it is? Time for noogies!"

I tried to smile, but it's hard to do when somebody is rubbing his knuckles on your head.

Gordon met me at the door and showed me around his house. We saw the place where he broke the lamp and the place where he threw up. Plus, he showed me something with little green and red lights, called a burglar alarm.

Then we went past an all-white room that was blocked off.
"That's the living room," he said. "Kids are never supposed to go in there alone. Things could get ugly. Want to see it?"
He grabbed my arm and pulled me inside.

There were monsters everywhere!
A chair grew long arms and reached out to grab me. The rug rolled up and turned into a giant snake. As I ran by, a lamp bent down and tried to eat me alive!

I looked up. Instead of seeing monsters, I saw Gordon's mom who looked pretty mad.

"Gordon, you know you're not supposed to be in here!" she yelled.

"It was Bobby's fault," whined Gordon. "He made me do it!"

She stared at me and then read a long list of house rules. I was starting to get a funny feeling about this sleepover.

For dinner that night we had some mushy green stuff. I didn't want to eat it, but one of the house rules was to clean your plate. Just as I finished the last bite, Gordon leaned over and plopped his food onto my plate.

"You should have eaten your vegetables, Bobby," said Gordon's mom. "See what a nice job Gordon did? He gets ice cream, but there's no dessert for you."

When I went to take a bath, Gordon popped up from the tub and soaked me with a water pistol. Then he ducked out of sight just as his mom came in.

"I'm disappointed in you, Bobby," she said. "Now, clean up this mess and go right to bed."

I had to escape.

In the middle of the night, I made my break. But just as I was climbing down from the bunk bed, I heard a voice.

"Going somewhere, Bobby?" It was Gordon.

"Uh, just to the bathroom," I croaked.

He told me, "It's down the stairs, past the little green light."

I raced my engine and roared off. Behind me, the prison
guards jumped on their motorcycles and came after me.

I drove down a dirt road and through a field, where my
path was blocked by a barbed-wire fence. There was just
one way to freedom — up and over the fence!

Suddenly, a loud siren went off.

Okay, I wasn't really in a field. I was in Gordon's hallway. The siren was coming from the burglar alarm. I guess I made it go off when I walked past the little green light, the way Gordon told me to.

Suddenly there were people everywhere — Gordon, his mom and dad, even a police officer. And they were all staring at me!

"Arrest me," I pleaded with the officer. "Take me anywhere but here!"

He wouldn't do it.

We both went back to bed. I hid under the covers for the rest of the night. When I woke up the next morning, I peeked out. Gordon was gone. "Hello," I called. No one answered.

Then it hit me. I was home alone in somebody else's house. I could do anything I wanted!

I marked up the walls with a huge crayon. I filled the bathroom with shaving cream. I dipped my feet in paint and ran across the carpet.

Well, at least that's what I thought about doing. What I really did was run downstairs and open the front door. Uncle Ted was standing there.

"Get me out of here!" I yelled.

"First we've got to thank Gordon and his family," he said. "Look, they're right behind you."

They were all sitting in the living room!

"We always spend Sunday morning in here," Gordon's mom explained. "It's one of our house rules."

After I got home, there was a knock at the door. It was Gordon and his mom.

"Bobby," said Gordon's mom, "I just wanted to thank you for being the only boy who ever stayed the whole night with Gordon."

"Well, for corn sakes, isn't that nice," my mom said. "Why don't we invite Gordon for a sleepover at our house tonight!"

I wanted to scream. Then I thought about it. Tonight would be different. Tonight Gordon would be on my turf.